AND SO TO BED

A
BEDTIME
COLLECTION

Compiled by Rita Storey

Illustrated by Pamela Venus

IDEALS CHILDREN'S BOOKS
Nashville, Tennessee

First published in the United States by
Ideals Publishing Corporation
Nelson Place at Elm Hill Pike
Nashville, Tennessee 37214

First published in Great Britain by
Beanstalk Books, Ltd.
The Gardens House, Hever Castle Gardens
Nr. Edenbridge, Kent TN8 7ND
England

Printed in Italy

ISBN 0-8249-8466-8

CONTENTS

To Win and Bob

Acknowledgments

Peggy Dunstan: "Hot Water Bottles." From *In and Out of the Windows* (Hodder and Stoughton Ltd.).
Eleanor Farjeon: "Bedtime." From *Silver Sand and Snow* (Michael Joseph).
Aileen Fisher: "After a Bath." From *Up the Windy Hill* by permission of the author, who controls the rights.
Roy Fuller: "Meetings and Absences." From *The World through the Window* (The Blackie Publishing Group).
Libby Hathorn: "Gone-Away Bear." Permission has been granted by the copyright holder Libby Hathorn, c/o Curtis Brown (Aust) Pty Ltd., Sydney.
Ogden Nash: "Sweet Dreams." From *Parents Keep Out* by permission of Curtis Brown, London, on behalf of the estate of Ogden Nash © Ogden Nash.
Pamela Rogers: "The Bedtime Thing."

Every effort has been made to trace copyright holders, but in a few cases this has proved impossible. The author and publishers apologize for these unwilling cases of copyright transgression and would like to hear from any copyright holders not acknowledged.

Up the Wooden Hill

Up the wooden hill
   to Bedfordshire,
Down sheet lane
   to blanket fair.

Author unknown

9

Let's Pretend

. . . that you are going on
     an exciting adventure

. . . that you are climbing a mountain

. . . that you are soaring and swooping like a bird

Go to Bed Late

Go to bed late,
    Stay very small;
Go to bed early,
    Grow very tall.

Author unknown

Bedtime

Five minutes, five minutes more, please!
  Let me stay five minutes more!
Can't I just finish the castle
  I'm building here on the floor?
Can't I just finish the story
  I'm reading here in my book?
Can't I just finish this bead-chain —
  It *almost* is finished, look!
Can't I just finish this game, please?
  When a game's once begun
It's a pity never to find out
  Whether you've lost or won.
Can't I just stay five minutes?
  Well, can't I stay just four?
Three minutes, then? Two minutes?
  Can't I stay *one* minute more?

Eleanor Farjeon

How do you go to sleep?

Do you sleep . . .

curled up
like a squirrel

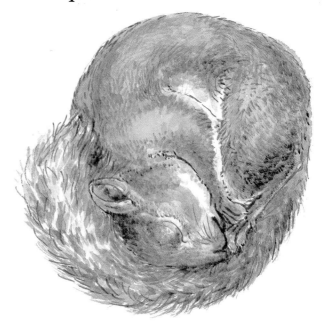

or a hedgehog

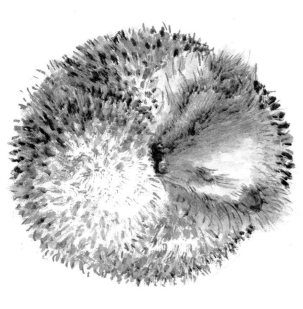

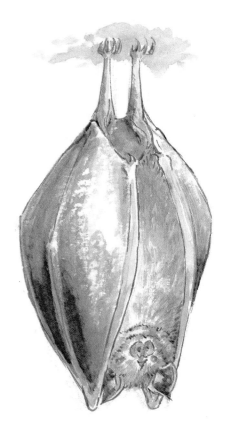

or upside-down like a bat?

Perhaps you sleep . . .

stretched out
like a puppy

or standing up
like a donkey?

Maybe you would rather be . . .

asleep while flying like this swallow . . .

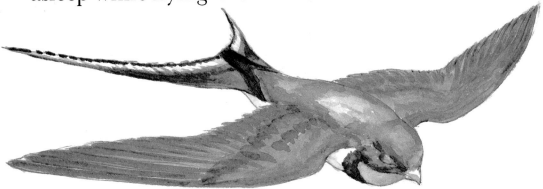

or maybe not?

How to Make a Mobile

Materials:

- Two 12-inch pieces of wire
- Strong thread:
  Four 8-inch pieces
  Two 5-inch pieces
- White posterboard or cardboard
- Crayons, paint, or felt-tip markers

Directions:

First, decide what kind of shapes you would like to hang on your mobile.
    Suggestions:
- moons and stars
- stars and spaceships
- sheep
- cow, moon, dish, and spoon
- cars and trucks

In order to balance the mobile, you will need to make your shapes roughly the same in size. Draw five shapes on the posterboard. Cut them out and either color or paint them. If you use paints, leave the shapes in a safe place to dry while you follow the next step.

Next, the centers of the two wires should be twisted together, as shown.

Bend the wires to make a criss-cross (+) frame. Tie one short string to the center of the frame to use for hanging.

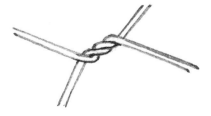

When your shapes are dry, make a small hole at the top of each one. Match each shape with a piece of thread, using the short thread for the center shape. Tie the short string to the center shape and attach underneath the middle of the frame. In the same manner, attach the other shapes to the ends of the wires.

Hold the mobile up by the hanging thread to make sure it is evenly balanced. Choose a place in your room, such as the ceiling or in front of a window, where you can hang the mobile so that you can see it from your bed.

Hot Water Bottles

It's comforting
   when winter's here
to have hot water bottles near,
providing
they are good and stout
and do *not*
let the water out.
   There's nothing good
that can be said
of leaking bottles
   in the bed,
not hot
   but cold and wet
               instead.

Peggy Dunstan

The Little Man Who Wasn't There

As I was going up the stair,
    I met a man who wasn't there.
He wasn't there again today.
    Oh! How I wish he'd go away.

Hughes Mearns

Gone-Away Bear

Libby Hathorn

I suppose when it all comes down to it, it was my fault that Amando got lost in the first place. To tell the truth, Amando's been a bit difficult lately – fighting, sulking, and even hiding from me.

Last week I found two of my dolls upside down in the fish tank and Amando sitting nearby with that angelic look on his hairy, little face. He refused to admit a thing, but I know very well that he did it! I shook Amando until his ears waggled, and then I shut him in the closet. I know that was a bit mean, but I thought he should be punished, so I left him lying there among the shoes. And that was

the last I saw of him – at least, I think that was the last I saw of him.

You see, I spent the night at a friend's house, and when I came home, I didn't really think about Amando. Anthony had bought me some new building blocks, and I played with them all morning. It wasn't till the afternoon that I first missed Amando. I went to the closet to get him and he wasn't there.

"Amando," I said very sternly, "come out from wherever you are. I know you're there, so come out at once!"

But Amando didn't come out. In fact, there wasn't a sound in the room except for the gurgling of Anthony's fish tank which he lets me keep in my room now. I thought maybe Amando was angry about being left in the closet and was hiding in one of his familiar places. I checked under the bedspread, on top of the chest of drawers and on the windowsill. No Amando. So I checked all the other places too—in the drawers, under the bed, on top of the clothes cabinet—everywhere. But still no Amando. I asked Mom and Anthony, but they hadn't seen him for ages.

"Check downstairs," Mom suggested. "Last time I saw Amando, he was on your windowsill. He may have fallen out of the window."

I went downstairs to the yard at the back of our apartments and saw Rose Epping making chalk drawings on the sidewalk. "I've lost Amando," I told her.

"Yup," she said, not looking up from her drawing.

"Seen him?"

"Nope."

I looked over her shoulder at her drawing. It was a person, but I couldn't tell if it was a man or a woman.

"A TV was stolen yesterday from Martin's house," she said while heavily coloring the chalk face with bright pink stripes. "Whoever took Martin's TV could've gone into your house and stolen Amando too."

"Nah, Anthony works at home all day. Anthony would've heard. Anyway, Amando was hidden in the closet."

Rose Epping shrugged.

"Well, where *is* he?" she asked deliberately. "Where's Amando *now*?"

I couldn't answer, so I went back upstairs and made another search of my room.

"Are you sure you didn't move Amando, Mom?" I asked.

"Quite sure," Mom said.

"Are you sure no one's been in my room, like that pesky Peter from upstairs or a robber or someone?"

"No one," Mom said.

"No one's been here," Anthony assured me, "except us, and we didn't touch Amando. Don't worry, he'll turn up."

But he didn't.

"Amando's very lonely at night if he's not in my bed," I complained to Mom when she came to tuck me in that night.

"We'll have a really good search for Amando tomorrow," she promised, "and we'll find him."

"He'll be sad without me tonight," I told her. "Very sad. He's probably crying right now."

"We'll find him tomorrow," she promised again.

Later I lay in the dark thinking about Amando some-
where lost and alone. I knew he'd have a great big lump
in his throat, the kind that makes it hard to swallow. I
knew he'd be brushing away a tear or two and sniffing and
looking for the tissues. I couldn't find the tissues either.

Next day we hunted all through the house for Amando,

but there wasn't a trace – not a whisker.

"I'll be at the mall this afternoon," Anthony told me. "I'll buy you a new teddy bear, just like Amando."

"No thanks," I said, all choked up. Anthony's awfully nice but sometimes he doesn't seem to know things, like the fact that Amando is a rare and precious bear.

"Amando's been with us always," Mom explained to Anthony. "You can't just go out and buy a bear like Amando." She squeezed my hand quite hard.

"I guess we'll just have to keep looking then," Anthony said.

"Want to come and play with me?" It was Rose Epping at the door. "Hide-and-seek?"

"I can't come and play," I explained. "I'm looking for

Amando. He's still lost and I've got to—"

"Yeah, yeah," Rose Epping cut in, "but you can look for Amando *any time*. Let's play at my apartment *now*. Hide-and-seek, okay?"

Rose Epping blinked at me through her small round spectacles, and I hated her at that moment waiting at the door for me to play hide-and-seek. I wasn't going to play with her now, or ever!

"No," I said, turning away.

"Do you want a candy bar?" she asked. "At my apartment?"

I just love Rose Epping's apartment, especially the kitchen cabinets. Her parents keep candy bars and chips and other delicious things, and you can eat them anytime.

"Yes," I sighed, following Rose Epping to her apartment. After all, a candy bar would give me the energy to go on looking. "But I've got to find Amando *before* hide-and-seek."

"Okay," Rose Epping said, "I'll help you find him then."

But Rose Epping couldn't find Amando either. After we'd looked and looked, we decided to play hide-and-seek after all. I didn't want to think about the coming night and just how lonely Amando was going to be without me once again.

Playing hide-and-seek with Rose Epping is great fun because she always pretends to be a very good monster when she's coming to get you and makes you very scared. You can always hear her getting closer and closer because she breathes so heavily. "Coming and coming to get you," she says in such a quiet little voice that it sends shivers up and down your back. Sometimes I have to cover my mouth and bite my fingers I want to squeal so much.

"Coming and coming to get you." I could hear her out in the hall. I wasn't even thinking about Amando when I crawled under my bed to hide from Rose Epping.

I knew she was in the room because her breath was coming in short snorts. "Coming and coming to get you," she repeated in that soft little voice and I pressed up harder against the wall. I heard drawers opening and doors banging. Any minute I would see her upside-down face and her glasses shining severely as she bent over the bed intent on my hiding place.

I'll scream, I thought. I'll scream out loud.

And I stuffed my hand in my mouth as Rose Epping jumped on the bed and slowly lifted the sheet that dangled

down and hid me.

"Coming and coming to—"

But before she could finish, before she even saw me, I yelled so loud it was Rose Epping who jumped.

"AMANDO!" I yelled. "Amando, Amando, Amando's here!"

The sheet went up quickly, her upside-down face appeared and it wasn't frightening at all!

"*You* said you *looked* under your bed for Amando," she glared.

"I did. We all did. But look where he is!"

I waggled an orange hairy paw that hung down now between the wooden slats of my bedbase.

"You can't see him unless you're lying right *under* here. He got under my mattress somehow. Quick, help me get him out or he could be squashed to death."

One thing about Rose Epping, she always knows what to do in an emergency, and she helped me get the mattress off the little bear very quickly. We checked for broken bones but Amando was okay. And he was *awfully* glad to see me.

"Hey, Mom! Hey, Anthony!" I called. "Hey, anybody! I've found Amando! We've found Amando! Hey! Hey!" I was awfully glad too.

That night, after Anthony and Mom had kissed me good night, I had a long, serious talk with Amando. We both promised that we would never be mean to each other again, and I promised especially that I would never put him in my closet or in any other closet for that matter. Amando hugged me very tightly and I even had to brush away a tear or two from his hairy, little face. He was so glad to be back with me, safe and sound. I stroked his forehead and his soft leather nose and I knew he'd fall asleep in no time.

"Am I glad to see you!" I said to Amando over and over again until Mom called out from down the hall.

"For heaven's sake, go to sleep!"

Then I gave Amando an extra big hug and I did!

After a Bath

After my bath
I try, try, try
to wipe myself
till I'm dry, dry, dry.

Hands to wipe
and fingers and toes
and two wet legs
and a shiny nose.

Just think how much
less time I'd take
if I were a dog
and could shake, shake, shake.

Aileen Fisher

Let's Pretend

. . . that you are fighting
giant jellyfish

. . . fierce sharks

. . . and pirates

31

Down Sheet Lane to Blanket Fair

How to Make Finger Puppets

As you lie in bed, look down at the folds in your bedspread. What do you see? Do you see just bumps and hollows, or could they be mountains and valleys?

Use your imagination to create your very own country. Think about what sort of land you would like. You could have a fairytale kingdom, with castles, a dragon, and a fairy princess. Perhaps you would rather imagine another planet, with fierce monsters, strange aliens, and plants. There are no limits in creating your land.

Make some finger puppet characters for your landscape to act out your adventures. Ask an adult for help with this project.

Materials:

paper	scissors
colored felt	cotton balls
glue	scraps of yarn

Directions:

Trace your finger which you will use for your puppets on a piece of paper. Then make the tracing a half-inch larger all the way around. Using this shape as a pattern, cut pieces from the felt.

Next, put glue around the outer edges of one of the felt shapes and place another felt shape on top of it. Leave it to dry.

After the shape is dry, you can decorate it to make any character you like. Use cotton balls for beards and moustaches, yarn for hair, and leftover scraps of felts for eyes, noses, and mouths.

Wee Willie Winkie

Wee Willie Winkie runs through the town,
Upstairs and downstairs in his nightgown,
Rapping at the window, crying through the lock:
Are the children in their beds, it's past eight o'clock?

William Miller

Bed in Summer

In winter I get up at night
And dress by yellow candlelight.
In summer, quite the other way,
I have to go to bed by day.

I have to go to bed and see
The birds still hopping on the tree,
Or hear the grown-up people's feet
Still going past me in the street.

And does it not seem hard to you,
When all the sky is clear and blue,
And I should like so much to play,
To have to go to bed by day?

Robert Louis Stevenson

There Were Five in the Bed

There were five in the bed and
  the little one said: Roll over! Roll over!
So they all rolled over and one fell out;

There were four in the bed and
  the little one said: Roll over! Roll over!
So they all rolled over and one fell out;

There were three in the bed and
  the little one said: Roll over! Roll over!
So they all rolled over and one fell out;

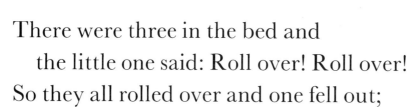

There were two in the bed and
   the little one said: Roll over! Roll over!
So they all rolled over and one fell out;

There was one in the bed, and
the little one said:
Good, now I've got the bed to myself,
I'm going to stretch and stretch and stretch!

Author unknown

Twinkle, Twinkle, Little Star

Twinkle, twinkle, little star,
How I wonder what you are!
Up above the world so high,
Like a diamond in the sky.

When the blazing sun is gone,
When he nothing shines upon,
Then you show your little light,
Twinkle, twinkle, all the night.

Then the traveler in the dark,
Thanks you for your tiny spark,
He could not see which way to go,
If you did not twinkle so.

In the dark blue sky you keep,
And often through my curtains peep
For you never shut your eye,
Till the sun is in the sky.

As your bright and tiny spark,
Lights the traveler in the dark,
Though I know not what you are,
Twinkle, twinkle, little star.

Jane Taylor

Hey Diddle Diddle

Hey diddle diddle,
The cat and the fiddle,
The cow jumped over the moon;
The little dog laughed
To see such sport,
And the dish ran away with the spoon.

Mother Goose

Shadows on the Wall

If you put your hand between a lamp and a wall in a dark room, it will cast a shadow. By following these pictures, you can turn the shadow into different animals.

Try to make up a story about some of the animals that you have created.

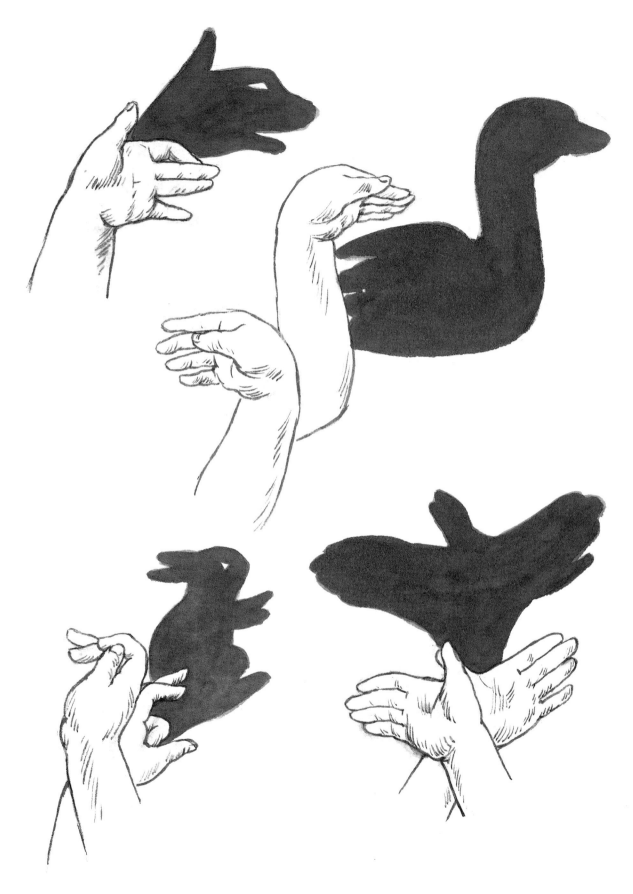

Let's Pretend

. . . to be an elephant

. . . to be a stork

42

. . . to be a clown in a circus

The Bedtime Thing
Pamela Rogers

Once there were two brothers named Jimmy and Mark. Jimmy was four and Mark was nearly two. Mark looked like a nice brother to have, with black hair and sparkly blue eyes. But there was one thing he would not do—he would not go to sleep at night.

Jimmy and his mommy and daddy waited and waited and hoped and hoped that one day he would go to sleep at night, but he didn't. So Mommy decided to take him to the clinic.

The lady in the white uniform looked at him.

"What a fine, handsome boy," she said.

"Mark may be a fine, handsome boy," said his mommy, "but we are worn out. He will not settle down at night. If he does go to sleep, he wakes up again and wants to get in our bed."

"Oh dear, dear," said the lady in the white uniform. "Do you have a night-light for him?"

"Yes," said Mommy.

"Does he still take a nap in the afternoon?"

"Yes," said Mommy, "for a little while after his lunch."

"Then give up that nap. He will then be so tired that he will sleep well. Give your mommy a rest, won't you?" she said to Mark, smiling.

"No," said Mark, and he hit the lady on the nose with his fist.

The lady stopped smiling, and Mark's mommy got up quickly and left with him.

After that she tried to keep Mark awake all day. He was glad not to take his afternoon nap. But by four o'clock, he was fussy and horrible.

"I'm worn out in the daytime *and* in the nighttime. What can we do, Jimmy?" said Mommy.

But Jimmy did not know. When Daddy came home he said, "Throw him out of the window."

He often said teasing things like this. But Mark didn't understand, and since he was already whiny and fussy, he began to howl.

"Now look what you've done," said Mommy. "A lot of help, you are!"

Daddy was sorry then, and gave Mark a piggyback ride to bed.

When Mark got into his crib, he fell asleep as soon as he was tucked in. They could hardly believe it. And Mommy read Jimmy a long story.

"Isn't it nice to have some time to ourselves, Jimmy?" she said.

No sooner had she said this, than Mark woke up. He was just as bad as ever.

So the next week, Mommy again took Mark down to the clinic. The same lady in the white uniform looked at Mark and told Mommy he was overtired.

"Give him a long rest in the afternoon," she said.

"Right," said Daddy crossly when Mommy told him. "It's we who are overtired, not him."

All that week, Mark had a long, long rest in the afternoon. He had no rest at night; nor did anyone else.

"Something has to be done," said Daddy. "Go down to that clinic again and ask to see the baby doctor."

So Mark's mommy did. The baby doctor examined Mark. She said he was a fine strong boy.

"*He* may be," said Mommy. "*I* am a nervous wreck."

She told the doctor all about Mark. But the doctor just tickled Mark under his chin and went on smiling.

"Never mind, Mother," she said. "Don't you worry. He will grow out of it."

This made Mommy very cross. She did not say anything more to the baby doctor, but all the way home, pushing the stroller, she was talking.

"It's all very well for her! He'll grow out of it! What about the rest of the family?"

She was walking so fast, Jimmy could hardly keep up with her.

"Perhaps he needs a Cuddly like me," he said.

Cuddly always slept in Jimmy's bed. He was a piece of furry material, and only Jimmy knew where his face was.

Because he had been with Jimmy for a long time, he seemed like a friend.

When Jimmy said this, Mommy stopped the stroller with a jerk.

"Jimmy," she said. "You are so smart! Of course! Mark needs a bedtime thing. All we have to do now is to find out what he would like!"

She was so pleased that she gave Jimmy a quarter for some candy. He bought some black, shiny licorice. Mark discovered he liked it too. Even when Mark's blue coat got wet, black, shiny pieces on it, Mommy went on smiling.

That night, she cut out another furry piece of material.

"Here you are, Mark," she said, as she tucked him in all cozy in his crib. "Here is a Cuddly, just like Jimmy's."

Mark looked at it. His mouth turned down. He picked up the new Cuddly and threw it on the floor.

"No," he said. "Mark not like it."

Mommy said, "I will tie it on the side of his crib. He may come to like it."

She tied it on with a piece of ribbon. When she was gone, Mark untied the ribbon and tied himself up in knots with

it. Then he howled more loudly than ever. So that would not do.

"I'll buy him a new teddy bear," said Daddy. "Anything for a peaceful night."

So the next day Daddy and Jimmy went out and bought a nice furry teddy bear for Mark. He was pleased with it and seemed to like it very much. But when it was bedtime, he pushed it out of his crib and began to cry.

"Oh dear," said Daddy. "Mark, I'm giving your new teddy bear to Jimmy."

Mark did not mind at all. He shouted more loudly than ever. He jumped up and down in his crib so much, that it rattled against the wall.

"We've got to be firm," said Daddy. "Mommy, Jimmy, we must leave him to cry."

He shut the door to Mark's room. They all listened to Mark crying. Jimmy did not like it. Nor did Mommy. Daddy liked it least of all. In a short time, he was stamping up the stairs again.

"Daddy!" said Mark in a pleased voice, when his door was opened.

"What will I do with you?" said Daddy.

Mark held out his arms, so Daddy picked him up and hugged him.

Mommy told Granny about Mark. She told all the aunts too. They began to make things for Mark at bedtime.

But although Mark played with them in the daytime, he did not want any of them as a bedtime thing. So at night, they lived on the shelf in Jimmy's room, so they would not be lonely.

One night when Jimmy was in bed, Mark was very bad. He threw one of his new bedtime things at the window of his room. This bedtime thing had a hard face. When it hit the window . . . Bang!

There was a tinkle of glass. Up the stairs ran Mommy and Daddy. They went into Mark's room.

"Now he's broken the window!" said Daddy.

"Oh, Mark!" said Mommy.

Mommy put her head around the door of Jimmy's room.

"Awake, Jimmy?" she asked. "What are we going to do now? Mark has broken his window. The rain's pouring in; he can't possibly sleep there."

"Put him in here," said Jimmy.

"Would you mind?" said Mommy.

Jimmy said he didn't mind. So Mommy put Mark back in his crib. Daddy came upstairs again. They panted and puffed as they pushed the crib through the hall. It got stuck in the doorway of Jimmy's room.

"Pull," said Daddy.

"Push," said Mommy.

"Beep! Beep!" said Mark.

At last Mark's crib, with him in it, was pushed through the door. It fitted nicely in the corner of Jimmy's room. Mark stood up in his blue pajamas with feet. He looked at Jimmy.

"Jimmy," he said.

"Oh dear," said Mommy. "I hope he doesn't keep Jimmy awake. If he does, we will have to move him in with us. Try to go to sleep."

She tucked Mark in, and turned out the light. She left the hall light on. Mark looked at Jimmy through the bars of his crib.

"Night night, Mark," said Jimmy.

"Ni, ni," said Mark, because he could not say "night" yet.

First one of his eyes closed, then the other. They opened once more to make sure Jimmy was there, then they shut again. Mark was asleep.

You will never guess what happened! He slept all night long! In the morning Mommy came in and said,

"I can't believe it! He must be getting sick."

She felt his head. She looked all over him for spots. But he was as well as could be!

"I don't mind having him here," said Jimmy. "He can sleep with me, if you want."

So the next night, Mark slept in Jimmy's room again. He was as good as gold.

Jimmy and Mark use Mark's old room as their playroom now—because you see, Mark found his bedtime thing—it was Jimmy!

The Sugar-Plum Tree

Have you ever heard of the Sugar-Plum Tree?
  'Tis a marvel of great renown!
It blooms on the shore of the Lollipop sea
  In the garden of Shut-Eye town.

Eugene Field

52

My Dream

I dreamed a dream a week from now,
    Beneath the apple trees;
I thought my eyes were big pumpkin pies,
    And my nose was Cheddar cheese.
The clock struck twenty minutes to six,
    When a frog sat on my knee;
I asked him to lend me fifteen cents,
    But he borrowed ten cents from me.

Author unknown

Would you rather sleep . . .

in a basket
    like a puppy . . .

in a burrow
    like a rabbit . . .

in a nest
    like a bird . . .

in a hutch
    like a guinea-pig . . .

in a hive
    like a bee . . .

in water
    like a fish . . .

in a stable
    like a horse . . .

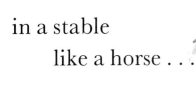

in a cave
    like a bear . . .

on a perch
    like a parrot?

Or perhaps you would rather sleep in your own bed
after all.

Meetings and Absences

How does your little toe
In the bed so long and bare,
Keep on discovering
The top sheet's little tear?

Roy Fuller

Sweet Dreams

I wonder as into bed I creep
What it feels like to fall asleep.
I've told myself stories, I've counted sheep,
But I'm always asleep when I fall asleep.
Tonight my eyes I will open keep,
And I'll stay awake till I fall asleep,
Then I'll know what it feels like to fall asleep,
Asleep,
Asleeep,
Asleeeep. . . .

Ogden Nash

Let's Pretend

. . . that you are as light as air,
like a bubble, drifting
up and up and up
toward the stars

. . . that you are on a
big ship, gently rocking
on the waves

. . . that you are floating up through the clouds on a
magic carpet

59

Good Night

Here's a body—there's a bed!
There's a pillow—here's a head!
There's a curtain—here's a light!
There's a puff—and so good night.

Thomas Hood

60

The White Seal's Lullaby

Oh! hush thee, my baby, the night is behind us,
    And black are the waters that sparkled so green.
The moon, o'er the combers, looks downward to find us
    At rest in the hollows that rustle between.
Where billow meets billow, then soft be thy pillow;
    Ah, weary wee flipperling, curl at thy ease!
The storm shall not wake thee, nor shark overtake thee,
    Asleep in the arms of the slow-swinging seas.

Rudyard Kipling